CRASHED

SCIENCE FICTION ROMANCE

KATE RUDOLPH

1

'LUXURY CRUISE LINER' was a stretch. Sarah's hair had been greasy since her first shower aboard Sky Chaser 4, and the stale stench of cannabis hung in the air no matter where she walked. But she was four hundred light years away from Earth and aboard a space ship! She couldn't be happier.

Winning the radio contest had seemed an impossibility when she entered, but the impossible hadn't stopped her from being born and it wasn't about to stop her from seeing the universe. Sure, her cabin didn't have a window. Sure, the ports of call were a bit... rough. And sure, her translator only understood about six of the twenty or more languages spoken by the passengers on the ship.

But none of that was going to get her down.

Not today. They were doing a flyby of a vacant planet, REX-9863, or Rex as the guidebook helpfully called it, and then they were going to Honora Station, the busiest trading post in this sector. She'd spy aliens that she'd never dreamed of.

Nearly two weeks earlier, on her first day on the ship, she'd been self-conscious about her conspicuous humanity. She'd been afraid that she'd be plain. Back home, no one noticed a dark haired, dark eyed, curvy girl with too much curiosity and mischief for her own good.

The Sky Chaser line catered mostly to bipedal, vocal species. But from the moment Sarah stepped aboard, she hadn't felt plain. Several of the incredibly buff warriors whose skin ranged from blue to dark purple stared at her wherever she went. Their ringleader, a devastatingly handsome purple man who was nearly two meters tall, had even opened the door for her to the entertainment deck.

Lithe, green men made eyes at her as she walked through the dining hall. And the pink women with bright yellow hair flirted and smiled, casually touching her whenever they could draw her into conversation here.

No, here she wasn't plain. For once, she felt like one of the pretty people. Or, if not pretty, then someone unique. After all, she was the only human on the ship. She'd been self-conscious for about a day, but then the strangeness began to feel ordinary. Everyone on the ship was an alien. Everyone was weird. And that just made her normal.

Sarah pulled on her swim suit and then covered that with a bright red jumpsuit. The upper deck pool would be the perfect place to watch the auroras on Rex. She'd knock back a few of the fruity drinks that made her head delightfully tilty and maybe work up the courage to talk to the purple warrior leader.

That was, if she could get him to step away from his friends for two seconds. That man never seemed to be more than a five meters from his own people. Clearly he hadn't settled into the same comfort that she had. But still, if Sarah worked up the nerve for it, she'd be happy to show him a little bit of Earthling hospitality.

What was a cruise light years from home good for if she didn't get some really memorable alien sex out of it?

That thought in mind, Sarah left her room

and headed for the pool. Sky Chaser 4 was huge and her room was located in the very bowels of the ship. She could hear the engine and life support system churning at all hours, but it had become white noise by now.

Sarah made it to the elevator bay without meeting another soul. She'd become accustomed to that. Despite its size, the ship could have taken on twice as many passengers as it seemed to have now with room to spare. As far as she could tell, she was the only person occupying a room in her hallway, and possibly the only person on the entire floor.

She'd just pressed the button for the elevator when a siren blared: three short pulses followed by a long, bleating honk. Sarah's heart kicked up and she looked around, but her eyes had trouble focusing on anything because of the red lights flashing from the ceiling.

Shit. What did that siren mean? She was either supposed to go directly back to her room or to go directly to one of the lifeboats. She looked around, hoping that she could follow someone else's lead. But she was still alone. She had to make the decision herself.

Life boat, she decided.

She took off, jogging back down the hall toward the emergency exit. The room through that door was barely warmer than freezing. She hugged herself and rubbed her arms over the thin fabric of her jumpsuit. The heating system clearly didn't reach this far.

Every level of the ship was equipped with a dozen or more life boats. They were located behind thick steel doors with heavy lock wheels to make sure they stayed shut. Sarah had expected someone to be there to direct her into one of the boats, but still, she was alone.

Maybe she should have gone back to her room.

No. Now that she'd made the decision, she was certain it was right. The siren meant they were supposed to get off the ship. Something was wrong. She spun the wheel and heard metal clank inside the door. With a tug, she pulled it open and stepped inside the dark escape vessel.

The life boat was little more than a narrow tube with benches bolted to either wall. The only thing to demarcate the seats were the restraints bolted above them. Sarah strapped herself in and waited, watching the door and trying to listen past the sound of the siren to see or hear if anyone would join her.

Minutes passed.

Then more minutes.

Still she was alone.

The siren cut off abruptly and her ears rang with the sudden silence. Was the threat over? Had this just been a drill? Sarah decided to give it one more minute before crawling out of the life boat and heading back to her room. She was barely keeping the catastrophic thoughts at bay, and now was not the time to think about the various reasons for the alarm to cut off.

She heard footsteps tromping down the hallway outside and two low voices arguing urgently. Her translator didn't understand the words. Not for the first time, she cursed the sub-dermal device.

The door slammed open and the purple warrior that she'd been eyeing for days stumbled in. He looked around, eyes darting to every corner, his brows drawn down in a harsh expression.

When he saw her sitting down, strapped to the wall, he let out an honest to God growl that did things to her private places. Sarah shivered. But any nascent fantasies were dashed when he turned around and banged on the door, yelling in that alien language. She didn't need a translator to know that he was cursing at whoever had locked him in.

Sarah was just about to speak up, but the escape vessel lurched. Her stomach jumped into her throat and she held on tight to the straps holding her in place as the gravity disengaged.

They'd been jettisoned and their life boat was falling through space.

2

SARAH LOST consciousness at some point during the fall. She didn't come to until the impact of the vessel crash landing jolted her against her restraints, the soft fabric digging in hard enough to bruise. Other than that pain, she was uninjured.

The purple warrior hadn't been as lucky.

He lay in a heap across from her, his body contorted into an almost impossible position. At first she feared him dead, but his chest rose and fell steadily as he sucked in breaths.

Unconscious, but alive.

For a moment Sarah wavered between checking on the unconscious warrior or checking out where they'd landed. She settled on leaving him be for the moment. She was awake and had her wits about her. If Rex was dangerous, she couldn't be trying to protect an injured man at the same time.

She took a deep breath and unhooked the restraints which held her in place. The sudden lack of tension hurt even more than the pressure had, and she swung her arms back and forth for a few seconds to try and get blood flowing.

Sparing one last look for the warrior, she approached the door. She looked out the little porthole above the window, but she couldn't see much. It was too bright.

From her quick read of the guidebook, she knew that Rex had a breathable atmosphere and a climate she could survive. She had to assume the same would hold true for her purple friend. She hadn't seen any life support suits inside the vessel. She had nothing to give him to help if he needed it.

She cranked open the door and looked out.

She could hear birds chirping and water lapping against land. It smelled of salt air with something faintly sweet and fruity woven through it. The air of Rex filled her lungs and she felt a little dizzy. It smelled so much *better* than the ship.

She'd forgotten that rusted metal and weed were not normal things to breathe in.

She leapt down from the door and landed in soft sand. Her feet sank into the hot granules and she wished that she was barefoot so that she could feel it between her toes.

Not now, she reminded herself. Despite the beauty of this spot that they'd landed on, the Sky Chaser cruise guide made it clear that the ship would not and could not land on Rex under any but the direst of circumstances. Help might be a long time coming.

She and her purple warrior were in danger. Sarah just didn't know what kind.

They'd landed on a beach. Behind the ship, reddish orange water stretched all the way to the horizon. A yellow sun shone high above them and the life boat's door faced a jungle of green and purple trees, the leaves fat and hanging down nearly to the ground. A bright blue bird sat atop one of those trees. It leveled its gaze at her and Sarah had the strangest feeling that it was sizing her up.

It let out a cry and took off, flying toward the interior of the jungle.

Sarah let out a breath.

Other than the bird, she saw no other living things. Wind whispered through her hair, deceptively cool. It wasn't quite warm enough that she wanted to swim; besides, the color of the ocean made her wary. At home on Earth, red water would have been toxic.

She walked around the life boat and took stock. The dark hull was covered in scorch marks along the bottom from where it had broken through the atmosphere. It was warm to the touch. There were markings above one of the seams in the side wall. Under them Sarah spotted a handle and a small depressor lock. She pressed the depressor and pulled on the handle.

A compartment in the life boat opened to reveal a dozen or so survival packs. They'd have food and water for days along with temperature controlled tents to keep them warm if the nights got too cold. Sarah said a silent thanks to any god that might have been listening and closed the compartment back up. They could unload it later.

It was safe enough for the moment. Safe enough to recover the warrior. She turned and walked back to the entrance of the life boat to find the warrior standing there scowling.

"You're awake!" It wasn't the ideal greeting,

but seeing him standing wedged in the doorway shocked any politeness out of her.

The warrior stepped out of the doorway and took two lurching steps toward her. He advanced until less than a meter separated them and she could smell the delicious masculine scent embedded deep in his skin.

The warrior raised a hand and cupped her cheek, his fingers sliding until they rested right behind her ear. For a moment Sarah thought he was going to kiss her. Then he started pressing behind her ear and she got even more confused.

"What are you—"

"Hush!" he said without moving his fingers.

This was one of those moments when Sarah realized that it was more prudent to stay still. The warrior towered over her, and he could have crushed her head between his beefy hands. His biceps were bigger than both of her arms put together. Suddenly, she was afraid. Rex might not have been dangerous so far, but this warrior could do her serious harm and there was no one but her to stop him.

With a final press of his index finger, he pulled back. Sarah's ears rang and she felt something click into place behind her ear. Her subdermal translator.

The warrior stepped back and nodded. "Much better."

Sarah took her own step backward, trying to put a decent amount of space between them in case he got other ideas. "What did you do?"

"Misconfigured translator." He waved at his ear in a circle. "It made a hell of a buzzing sound. I fixed it."

Without meaning to, she raised her hand to the spot he'd just touched. She could feel the small protrusion of the implant under her skin. Stranger still, she could almost feel the imprint of his fingers. It was like he'd marked her somehow.

She gulped.

Sarah wanted to take another step back, but that felt too much like running away. Sure, he'd touched her, but he hadn't tried to hurt her. Yet. No, she wouldn't worry about it. They had bigger problems.

The warrior studied her, the shocking blue of his eyes enough to send shivers down her spine. But they weren't cold. A raging inferno of heat swirled in them, intense enough to scald her. She'd thought him attractive from afar, but looking into his eyes, she could see that he was dangerously beautiful.

"Are you injured?" he asked, unaware of the turn her thoughts had taken.

"No, I'm okay." She'd been moving around and nothing felt injured. Sure, she was sore and bruised, but there was nothing she could do about it at the moment. And she wasn't the person to be worried about. At least she'd been strapped into the life boat when it ejected. "What about you?"

His dark brows drew down and his eyes narrowed. "I am well."

She'd have dreams about the way his lips formed those words. Already her fingers itched to reach up and trace over the full burgundy skin. She'd heard lips described as sinful before, but she hadn't realized what that meant. Looking at this warrior's lips, she got it.

But she had to look beyond his lips. He wore low slung gray pants hanging off of his hips and a thin white shirt. It was so thin that she could make out the contours of his dark abs in shades of purples and burgundies. Sarah wanted to do wicked things to those muscles. There was a faint pattern to his skin, dark dots that she could barely make out. In all other ways, he looked a lot like a very purple human man.

Was it the same under his pants?

Sarah shook her head. She wasn't trying to ogle him, she was trying to figure out if he was concealing an injury. On the surface he *looked* alright, but with purple skin, she couldn't tell if he was covered in bruises or not. She wasn't even sure what color he would bruise.

She'd need to take him at his word for the moment. She moved on. The more time they wasted, the more time they'd be stuck on a deserted planet. "There might be a radio with the survival gear," she said. "Maybe we can get in touch with Sky Chaser 4 and they can send someone to help." Otherwise, they'd need to hike and hope they found civilization.

The warrior tilted his head to the side, doubt and bemusement written plainly on his alien skin. "Do you truly think they're in a position to do so?"

It was Sarah's turn to be confused. "We fell by accident, didn't we?" She hadn't spent any time figuring out why they were ejected. But what else could it have been? "Some sort of mechanical malfunction?" Whatever it was, they were lucky to be alive.

The warrior was not convinced. "I highly doubt that."

"Why's that?" she asked, truly curious.

"Because... never mind." He shook his head and took a deep breath, relaxing. As the tension drained from his muscles, he shrank by a few centimeters, still a head taller than her, but now much more like a large man than a terrifying warrior. "My name is Nyxant. Of Oscavia." He added the last bit as an afterthought.

So the warrior had a name. It was nice to know after all the time she'd spent thinking about him back on the cruise. Now she had something to call him while she dreamed.

Or not. She needed to get off this planet, not have crazy sex fantasies about a purple warrior named Nyxant.

"I'm Sarah Gallagher. Of Earth." She almost added Canada to where she was from, but thought better of it. Planetary politics of a barely interstellar backwater wouldn't be of interest to anyone outside of her solar system.

Nyxant looked over her shoulder out toward the

horizon. "Night will fall soon, Sarah." Her name on his lips made her shiver. He said it like no human, emphasizing the last syllable and breathing it out.

They had to make camp. And she needed to get a hold of herself. "I found supplies," she told him and led him around to the outside of the life boat. Rex's sun was setting fast and she could feel that it was going to be a cold night.

Hopefully by morning Sky Chaser 4 would realize that they'd been ejected. Otherwise, her vacation had just been extended indefinitely.

3

THE TENT KEPT her warm enough, but Sarah still woke before sunrise. By the time Nyxant began to move in his own tent, she'd started a fire and had boiled water from one of the survival packs to make tea. The rest of their breakfast would consist of bland nutrition bars, so she hoped that the drink would make up for it.

They had a long day ahead of them.

Her first task after she'd woken up to the pre-morning dark had been to go over every bit of survival gear they'd salvaged from the life boat. And this time it had paid off. She'd found a small solar powered transmitter that should be strong enough to radio Sky Chaser 4 for help. She would have done it already if she'd been able to get a clear signal from the beach.

So she'd fashioned two packs and stuffed them full of food and sundries. As soon as they were done eating, she and Nyxant would be off, walking up the hills, hopefully to their rescue. The days were short here and they'd need to leave soon if they hoped to reach high ground by nightfall.

The sound of a zipper being pulled down drew her attention. She looked over to see Nyxant's fingers pop out of his tent and prop open the thin, stiff material so that he could climb out.

He grabbed a cleaning towel from the supplies he'd gathered the night before and walked around to the broad side of his tent, where the brightest patch of rising sun gave him the best light.

Sarah had to bite her lip to keep her mouth from dropping open. He looked like he'd just rolled out of a plush bed after a night of wicked pleasure. His dark hair was tousled around his shoulders and face, but not tangled. There was a light sheen of sweat that seemed to make him glow.

How could a man look like that after the day and night they'd just had? Talk about unfair.

She turned back to heating the tea, afraid that she'd be caught staring. She poured hot water into two cups over the broken up leaves. The fragrant, earthy aroma wafted up into her nose and she took a deep breath, sucking it in.

Nyxant finished his washing and sat down on an overturned supply box beside her. She tried not to be disappointed when she saw that he'd put on a shirt. Silently, she handed him the tea and two nutrition bars. They had plenty of food and no reason to ration it just yet.

Nyxant placed the wrapped up nutrition bars in the sand beside him and cupped the tea mug in both of his hands. He stared down at it intently, taking deep breaths. His study was both sensual and contemplative.

"It's just tea," Sarah said, feeling self-conscious. It wasn't like she'd made anything special.

Nyxant looked up at her and then back down at the tea, eyes narrowed. He leaned forward, nose nearly touching the liquid, and took a deep breath. She could see the steam hitting his face and leaving a faint layer of dew.

He pulled back, sitting up straight, and reached into his pocket to retrieve a small metal rod no longer than his palm. He stuck it into the dark liquid and swirled it around a few times before pulling it out and casually examining the wet end.

After a moment, his face softened. He wiped the rod on his pants before sticking it back into his pocket. He raised the cup to his lips and drank deeply, ignoring that it was too hot to do any more than sip. "Thank you," he said when he put the cup down.

That had been a test for poison. She'd seen characters do things like that on media shows back home, but never in real life. What kind of person worried about a shipwrecked companion trying to poison them? Sure, she'd had concerns for *her* safety, but she was a woman alone and he was a gargantuan man.

He had nothing to fear from her. Was life on Oscavia so fraught? She wanted to ask him about his homeworld, but they didn't have time. She could ask him once they were safe. If they ever made it back.

Sarah picked up the small device that she'd sat on top of the pack at her feet. "I found a transmitter, but the signal is crap down here. I think if we head to higher ground," she said, pointing to the peak visible through the forest, which was at least ten kilometers away, "We might be able to get a message out."

Nyxant put his tea down. "Is the line secure?"

"Of course not." It was a simple transmitter, there was no way to secure the signal. And why would they care about that?

"Hmm." He unwrapped one of his nutrition bars and took a bite, not saying anything else.

"Do you have a better idea?" Sarah wasn't going to die on this forgotten rock. They only had a small timeframe to hope that Sky Chaser 4 was still within signal range.

Nyxant spoke slowly. "There is one spot on this entire planet that we can be traced to. I don't see why we should abandon it in some vain hope that a radio will provide our salvation." He picked at his nutrition bar and stared out at the water rather than looking at her.

"So you just want to sit here and wait to be rescued?" He didn't look like the type. No man who looked as much like a fighter as he did could stand to sit around for long. She wondered again if he'd injured himself in their landing. If he was cautious enough to test tea for poisons, maybe he wouldn't trust a stranger knowing his injuries.

"I suppose I do." Then he looked over, the expression on his face possibly meant to placate her. "As you suggested, we might have been victims of a system malfunction."

He hadn't changed his mind, she was sure of it. There was more to the story of how he'd gotten here. "Who put you in the life boat?" she asked.

That threw him. "Excuse me?"

She'd had a few hours to unwind and think about what had happened. And some things weren't making sense. "I thought the alarm meant to go to the life boats, but clearly it didn't. You, though, were put into it by someone. They locked you in. Why?"

His face closed off, as expressionless as a mask. "That is none of your concern."

"I'm not an idiot, okay?" And she didn't need to be coddled. All Sarah wanted to do was to get off this damned planet and back on her vacation. Though she doubted that she'd have a comfortable moment after being ejected in a possibly faulty escape vessel. Maybe it would be time to disembark for good at the next *actual* landing point.

But she wasn't going to get caught up in whatever mess of a life Nyxant had. He could have his secrets and his personal drama. She didn't want to deal with it.

"I did not mean to imply anything of the sort," he said, almost sounding apologetic. There was a strange cadence to his voice, formal and stilted. The translators sometimes added a layer of awkwardness, but this was beyond that. He spoke far more carefully than a man in danger should.

But she wasn't worrying about that now.

Sarah stood and wiped off some of the sand that had somehow gotten on her shirt. She slung one of the packs over her shoulders and secured the straps. "I'm not risking getting left here," she told him. "If the ship leaves, it could be months— *if we're lucky*—before another one wanders through this corner of space. I'm going to signal the ship." And she'd do it alone if she had to.

Nyxant didn't have a problem with that. He leaned back on the box, resting his arms behind him, and said, "Best of luck," with a small smile and a nod of his head.

It wasn't wise to go alone. She knew it. But the need to *move* seized her. If they stayed on the beach, they wouldn't be found. She had no idea why he didn't want to move. She didn't buy his story about staying in the one place they could be tracked to. Maybe he was injured, but if he wouldn't tell her, she couldn't help him.

She was done debating.

Sarah tossed the second pack that she'd prepared toward Nyxant. It landed at his feet. "In case you decide to join me," she explained.

Nyxant simply waved her on and said, "Good luck."

She shook her head and muttered, "Whatever."

Sarah climbed up the incline of the beach to the edge of the jungle. There was an opening between two trees, but the dense leaves brushed against her, leaving a sticky sap on her jumpsuit. She was thankful her arms were covered. The sap smelled sickly sweet, but there was an under-tone of something vinegary and rotten. She breathed through her mouth to try and block out the scent.

There wasn't a jungle this dense back on Earth. Not one that any human was allowed in, in any case. Greenery and Carbon Recovery Zones were strictly regulated for the health of the planet.

So to see the trees growing high overhead and blotting out the sun was something else. It was barely bright enough to see by the light that filtered through the leaves. Birds chirped and leaves rustled from a faint breeze that she could hear but not feel. Her head tilted up, trying to see through the canopy above her, but it was a solid ceiling of branches and leaves in brilliant hues.

She tripped over a thin vine snaking across the ground and stumbled. It was warning enough that Sarah needed to stop gawking and pay attention to the space in front of her. After walking for several minutes, Sarah's calves started to ache. She was headed uphill, even though the jungle looked flat for as far as she could see.

There wasn't a path, but Sarah thought she was headed in the right direction. She paused to give her legs a little rest. Gravity weighed heavy on her. It just wasn't the same in space, no matter what artificial gravity drives tried to reproduce. She spotted a nice, long, sap free stick and picked it up. It would work as a walking staff.

When she looked back toward the direction she'd been heading, her head spun. *Was* this the direction that she'd been heading? Every way she looked, the trees appeared the same. She could not tell north from south or east from west. And even if she'd been able to see the sun, she couldn't guarantee the directions would be the same as they were on Earth.

She should have never gone alone.

Sarah pulled the transmitter out of her bag and flipped it on. For a moment, hope sprung up in her as it scanned for a signal. A blue line glided from one side of the small screen to the other, but after thirty seconds, it flashed three times and then went dark. No signal.

Damn it.

She needed to keep moving. Sarah took a deep breath, the humid air of the jungle filling her lungs. She let her eyes drift shut and tried to center herself as if one small moment of meditation would give her the sense of direction she needed.

The hairs on the back of her neck stood up. Then her arms broke out in gooseflesh.

She was being watched.

It was impossible to know how she knew it, other than by some inborn instinct. She could feel a pair of eyes on her, tracking her every move.

Sarah wanted to freeze and dive for cover. She didn't know what danger Rex held, and she didn't want to find out.

Instead, she kept moving. The feeling of being watched didn't dissipate, but she kept her ears and eyes alert for any sign that she was being followed. After several minutes, there was nothing.

She couldn't shake the feeling that there was something behind her, but Sarah tried to keep it together. As far as she knew, she and Nyxant were the only people on this corner of the planet. Possibly the only people on the planet at all. The only person that could be watching her was him.

Had he followed her?

She almost called out for him, but the words died in her throat. Something wrapped itself around her leg and jerked, sending her flying off her feet and dragging her into the underbrush.

Sarah screamed.

4

DIRT AND FALLEN twigs scraped against her face as Sarah was pulled across the rock strewn ground. By some miracle she was able to keep hold of the stick she'd grabbed onto earlier. She tried to strike out and use it to wedge herself into place, but she couldn't get purchase. The slimy thing wrapped around her foot yanked, and she flipped over and was pulled quickly along her back rather than on her stomach.

She beat at it, hitting her leg more than the ugly, slimy black arm wrapped around her. Suddenly, they stopped and Sarah lurched forward. She pulled herself back just in the nick of time. Another tentacle flew toward her, curling briefly around the thin trunk of a young tree before letting go, leaving a trail of dark slime in its wake.

Sarah tried to scurry back, but the tentacle might as well have been made of solid iron. She could barely move her leg from side to side, and she couldn't inch backward or forward. She grasped her stick and tried to wedge it between the black, sucker coated skin and the red material of her jumpsuit. She sucked in a deep breath and gritted her teeth as the wood dug deep into her calf, bruising her.

Goddamn, it hurt.

But she kept going. She didn't know why they'd stopped and she didn't want to go any further. That was *it*. The second she got free she was going to run back to the beach and sit next to Nyxant until Sky Chaser 4 found them or they ran out of food. Either of those options was better than being eaten—hopefully *only* eaten—by an alien tentacle monster.

The stick slid under the tentacle and she let out a little gasp in success. It turned into a dejected yowl when the tentacle rippled and started to move up her calf, the pointed end leading the way in a very, *very* gross and suggestive march.

Nope. She'd cut her leg off before she let it get any further.

If only she had a knife.

Sarah tried to kick, and when that failed, she tried to use her heel to push the creeping tentacle down. It didn't work, not exactly, but the arm did stop its crawl. It didn't retreat, though. One of its suckers latched onto her shoe.

Why had she been so insistent on coming here alone? She should have talked this through with Nyxant. Maybe if she had waited five goddamn minutes, he would have come around. Or maybe he would have convinced her to stay.

Something glinted in the oozing black mass of tentacle as a wickedly sharp stinger slowly pulsed out of the shiny skin. It grew, centimeter by centimeter, until it was as long as Sarah's hand and as thick as one of her fingers. Something bright green seeped from the end, and she knew that it couldn't bury that thing in her. If it did, she was a goner.

But her eyes were transfixed. The tentacle reared back, though it was long enough that it could still wrap around her leg tightly. It didn't strike quickly, almost like it could sense her fear and savored the taste.

She couldn't watch. Even as she struggled, she got nowhere. Sarah slammed her eyes closed, as if not being able to see the attack would save her from it.

There was a loud thump beside her and the tentacle on her leg went slack.

Sarah opened her eyes and saw Nyxant crouching beside her, a wickedly long knife in his hand covered in green goo. Without waiting for his command, she pulled her leg, the tentacle a heavy dead weight around it. She reached forward, peeling it off until she was free. Nyxant crouched beside her, looking deep into the bushes where the creature had to be lurking.

"Can you run?" he asked, voice pitched low.

"Yes," she answered, heart hammering in her chest.

Something rustled within the trees. Sarah scampered to her feet, hissing in pain when she put weight on her right leg, the one the tentacle had been wrapped around. Something felt wrong with it, but they had to move.

Nyxant threw his arm around her shoulders and they were off. She had no idea which direction they were going in, but she let Nyxant lead.

He seemed to intuitively understand the lay of the land.

Every step was agony. Sarah had to bite her lip to keep from crying out. When that didn't work, she tried to control her breathing through her mouth. She didn't know if the monster had crushed something or if she was merely severely bruised, but she couldn't go on for much longer.

The jungle was too dense to run fast for long. After a few minutes, Nyxant slowed to a light jog, dodging under low branches in a fluid motion and taking her with him, guiding her as if she were boneless.

She didn't know how long they walked. The pain in her leg grew and grew until time lost meaning, and all Sarah could do was focus on the step in front of her. She was terrified that if they stopped, the thing that had grabbed her would take her again. She wanted to ask Nyxant how he'd found her and why he'd come, but opening her mouth at all would let the whimper she was holding back escape.

Nyxant's arm was a constant presence, propping her up and keeping her grounded. If he hadn't kept moving, she doubted she would have been able to. But he moved in silence and without complaint. She could do the same. She had to.

Finally, after what seemed like years, she heard the distant lapping of water against the shore. The beach. They were back to the ship. It took a few more minutes, but they made it through. The trees gave way to sand and sun.

Nyxant dropped his arm from around her shoulders. Sarah tipped forward, not even caring that she fell. She was safe.

When Nyxant fell right beside her, she knew something was terribly wrong.

5

AT FIRST SARAH thought Nyxant had fallen over from exhaustion. That would have been bad, but on a scale of one to ten, it only rated a two and a half. But when she rolled to her side to get a good look at him, she saw that his face had lost a lot of color, fading from a magnificent deep purple to lilac.

That looked more like a seven.

She crawled over to him, the action much less painful than walking, and tried checking for a pulse. Only as her fingers hovered over his neck did she realize that he might have a completely different circulatory system than she did.

The moment of hesitation cost her. Nyxant's hand clamped around her wrist and his eyes popped open, a demon lurking behind his irises. He snarled and growled, but when his eyes met hers, the monster bled out of them and his grip relaxed, though he didn't let her go.

"Men have died for less, *cavria*." The words were a threat, but the way he said that last word sent a pleasurable shiver down her spine. She wondered what *cavria* meant. If her translator hadn't interpreted it, it meant there wasn't a simple definition in English.

"You kill people who are trying to make sure you're alive? You sure are a bag of fun." She pulled her hand back and he let her go. She might have been crouched over him, but there was a coiled power inside Nyxant that made her think that if he wanted her to stay still, he could make her. She spied darkly bruised skin under a tear in his shirt, but sensed that he would not like her to touch him. Not yet.

"Life is full of danger," was his response.

"No shit." Sarah rolled back over to sit beside him. She pushed up her pant leg all the way to her knee to see the damage that the tentacle had done to her. It wasn't pretty. A dark mark snaked up, the skin bruised and even more purple than Nyxant's. No wonder walking had been so tough.

She looked from her ankle to the alien beside her. "Thank you for saving my life," she said, suddenly serious. Seeing the injury hit home just how much danger she'd been in.

He was quiet for a long moment, his eyes deep with something dark that she could not describe. Another moment passed between them before he said, "You are the only other person here. If you die, I'll go mad for want of company."

The way he said *want* did things to her. Things that she couldn't do with a bum leg and an injured man. But now there was something more than simple lust. If he'd propositioned her that morning, she would have slept with him. He was beyond hot and she'd had her eye on him for weeks.

Now things had changed. He'd saved her life, and she was beginning to spot a reservoir of something hidden beneath his warrior exterior. She wanted—*needed*—to learn more about this man. She could feel it in her bones.

But to do that, she'd need to ensure that he made it through the night. The medkits were back by the rest of the supplies. She could see the shape of their tents near the water, and if she could walk, she'd be there and back in under a minute. But her ankle throbbed, and walking was out of the question.

Crawling wasn't.

It took a little experimenting, and her knees were not going to thank her, but Sarah was able to get herself over to the supply chest and grab one of the simple medkits that had been included in their provisions. She slung the strap over her shoulders and let it fall on her back while she crawled back toward Nyxant.

He lay flat on his back with his head angled to the side so he could watch her move, a laughing smile lighting up his face.

"What?" Sarah knew she didn't look sophisticated, but she'd made it work.

Nyxant didn't stop grinning. "You look—it amuses me."

Under other circumstances she might have been offended. She slid the kit around and held it up toward him and said, "Keep laughing at me and I'll use this medkit on myself and let you suffer."

That got a true laugh out of him. It came from deep within his chest, surprising a loud burst of air out of his lungs. And then he was clutching his side and gasping, the mirth a wounding blow.

"That monster didn't do this to you." It had been so focused on her that he'd barely needed to fight it off.

Nyxant sucked in shallow breaths as she used a knife in the kit to cut away the remains of his shirt. "No, I'm afraid that was our rough landing," he said.

Things were starting to make sense. She'd suspected that he may have been injured, but not this badly. "And is that why you didn't want to traipse through the jungle?"

"Predominantly, yes," he conceded.

"And you couldn't have just said you had broken ribs?" She would have never fought to leave if he needed medical treatment. She pulled out a container of healing solution. It was a bright blue salve which healed non-life-threatening injuries in most carbon-based species. On Earth, it was also worth ten times its weight in gold.

"They were merely bruised at that point," he explained.

Nyxant hissed as she rubbed the cool liquid against his injured skin. She could feel a bump on his side where his ribs should have been smooth and covered with muscle. It took several minutes and all of the solution, but the nasty bruise was covered with the thick blue goo.

"Nyxant..." Her fingertips rested on his rippled muscles. His skin was so warm and soft under the heat of the sun.

Nyxant reached up and cupped her cheek, tilting her face toward his. "I like the sound of that name on your lips," he said.

Those blue eyes of his were dangerous. Sarah could feel herself falling into them as she leaned forward. She wouldn't need to move much to taste him.

But she pulled back. "You should be all good in half an hour," she said. She looked down at the small tub, hoping that there was a little scoop left for her to use on her leg. But she was out of luck. His chest was far too broad for her own good, in more ways than one.

She looked back over her shoulder. It was a trick of the light, but their campsite looked like it had moved a kilometer or two down the beach. She took a deep breath and prepared herself for the crawl.

Nyxant stopped her with a hand on her arm. "Hold still, *cavria*," he insisted. "Once my wounds have set, let me tend to yours." He paused.

"Unless the pain is too bad. I would not have you suffer merely so I could have the pleasure of tending to you."

Tending her would give *him* pleasure? If it was an excuse to get his hands on her, she'd wait for hours. "It's not that bad if I don't move." As she settled back down next to him, she knew she *almost* wasn't lying. It hurt, but she could manage.

She expected him to let go of her wrist, but he slid his hand down until their fingers were entwined. His thumb circled lazily against her skin. "I have not had so much fun in quite some time," he admitted.

"I'm glad my near death experience was enjoyable for someone." The wry words just slipped out.

He tried to explain. "Following you—"

She interrupted, "Stalking, you mean?" She was laughing as she accused him, their conversation causing her pain to fade into the background of her thoughts.

"Stalking you, yes." He agreed and laughed a little. "On my home planet, there is a tradition."

"Isn't there always?"

He laughed again and Sarah got the idea that it wasn't something he got to do all that often when he wasn't stranded on a deserted planet. Then his smile faded and he said, "Never mind."

"No! I want to hear." She wanted him to laugh again, and the rumbly sound of his voice was the perfect distraction from the throbbing pain crawling up her leg.

"There is a tradition. A courtship tradition," he clarified. "When a couple intends to seriously consider a partnership, they will play a courtship game. One will journey into the least hospitable terrain possible, and the other goes on the hunt." He looked deep into her eyes as he described it, inviting her to imagine what that game would be like with him. "When the first is caught, they can choose to accept the affections of their pursuer."

Affections? There was only one thing that could mean. "Sounds kind of... cavemanny." She wanted to ask if the guy had to carry around a huge club to knock out the competition. But when she imagined Nyxant chasing after her, intent on seduction, she could understand the appeal.

"Cave...manny?" He didn't quite get the pronunciation right and she realized that the translator had failed.

"Um, barbaric?" she substituted.

He laughed again, the sound coming more

easily the more he did it. "I promise, it is mostly an excuse for some alone time. Courtship is a tedious process." He rolled toward her and rose above her, holding himself over her like a lover. "I do wonder if you would make the game worth it. If you knew you were playing."

Was he talking about the chase? Or courtship in general? Sarah wanted to ask, but an insidious thought niggled at her. Had he played that game before? If anything happened between them, would she just be another conquest? The words died in her throat before she could gather the courage to ask.

He wiped her hair out of her eyes and stood, loping over to their gear in easy strides as if his ribs hadn't been broken only moments before. When he got to his tent, he stripped off the tattered remains of his shirt, but he didn't bother to cover himself back up. He picked up another medkit and brought it back to her.

Sarah's mouth watered. The goo had seeped into his skin while it healed, leaving his chest shining and the same rich purple of the rest of him. God, he was magnificent.

He knelt at her feet and studied her leg, brows

drawn down in contemplation. "I don't think you're broken," he said.

"That's an entirely different conversation," she joked. One no magic healing goo could fix.

He looked up from her injury, expression curious. But he didn't ask the question. "This is going to hurt," he warned.

She nodded. Of course it would. Everything came with its price.

6

THE NEXT DAY, Sarah started early. She rolled her ankle around experimentally, testing for any tweaks or twinges. It was as good as new. Better than new, actually. A scar she'd had on the side of her leg for as long as she could remember had disappeared, replaced with baby smooth skin.

Nyxant stoked the fire while she gathered wood from the edge of the jungle. She eyed the dense trees warily, on the lookout for anything ready to snatch her up. But she was able to return to camp unmolested, her arms piled high with wood.

"Do you like fish?" Nyxant asked. Today he wore the pants he'd landed in and had cloth draped over his shoulders in something almost resembling a cloak. The one thing their survival packs lacked were clothes.

"Of course." She was already growing tired of the nutrition bars. If they were stuck here for long, she might sample the tree leaves just for a little flavor. And as of now, their fate was in the hands of Sky Chaser 4. She'd dropped the transmitter during her scuffle with the monster in the jungle. They had no way to communicate with anyone but each other.

Nyxant's toes curled in the sand. He'd chosen to forgo shoes. He smiled at her response. "Good. I think I can rig up one of the tents to act as a net. Perhaps we'll have a tasty dinner."

He set to work on one of their spare tents while Sarah arranged a woodpile by the fire. They worked in companionable silence. And if Sarah's eyes occasionally drifted over to study Nyxant's rippling muscles as he worked, she had nothing to be ashamed about. After all, more than once she caught him looking at her.

After a few hours, he stood up and stretched. The movement caught her eye. Nyxant put his whole body into it, arms outstretched and back arched, showing his alien features off to perfection.

God, she wanted to lick every inch of him.

All morning, desire had been an uncomfortable companion, making her hyper-aware of her own body and the tightening of her muscles down to her core. The wicked question of whether they were physically compatible kept flittering through her head. Nyxant may not have looked completely human, but their differences didn't seem so different right now.

And if human ingenuity was good for one thing, it was finding pleasure in the unknown.

As he headed out toward the water, she forced herself to look away and focus on the tasks that she'd set for herself. If she didn't start working, she'd spend the entire day staring at Nyxant. And she really, *really* wanted to. But she couldn't.

After finishing stacking up the wood, Sarah set about organizing their supplies. She had no idea how long they'd need to stay on Rex, and now she needed to tally up their food and medkits before they began to run low.

The job took longer than she thought. The sun beat down on her hard and sweat poured down her neck. She had no idea how much time had passed, but when she stood up, her muscles ached.

"I'm afraid my results have been less than fruitful." Nyxant's voice was close. She hadn't realized that he was standing right behind her.

Sarah turned around and froze.

He was naked. Very, very naked.

And any questions she had about biological compatibility evaporated. One quick glance before she could force herself to look away told her all she needed to know. They'd fit.

She couldn't keep her eyes from tracking up and down, drinking in every inch of him. Along the outer edges of his thighs she saw dark patterns in his skin where it thickened into a pointed ridge that ran from hip to knee. His legs and chest were dappled with darker purple spots, nearly black against his skin.

Before she could ogle him anymore, he wrapped a torn piece of cloth around his waist. "I'm sorry, my clothing got wet in the course of my endeavors."

"Not a problem." Her voice did *not* squeak when she said that. "So no fish?" she asked, desperate to change the subject.

"We can always try again tomorrow. I fear we now have an abundance of time." Nyxant stepped closer and Sarah could smell the salt of the water that had sunk into his skin. "Though I do not regret that I have the freedom to spend it with you."

Those blue eyes of his were trouble. If Sarah had been raised by a mother, she might have been warned about them. She wasn't sinking into them; instead, she felt speared, held utterly captivated like prey.

His eyes darkened, clouding with wicked intent as he cupped her cheek and leaned in close. It was a chaste kiss, his lips pressed gently against hers. Sarah's arms came up and wrapped loosely around his waist, her fingers gliding against his warm skin.

Her blood ran hot in her veins as his tongue traced the seam of her lips, begging for entrance. Sarah opened up to him, letting him explore her as she basked in the taste of him. Every caress was a revelation. Her skin prickled in awareness as his hands traced over the material of her jumpsuit, pressing down and feeling the outline of her curves.

Sarah arched up, practically purring as his hands traced lower, cupping her ass for a fleeting moment before he slid back up, leaving one hand on her waist and burying the other in her hair.

She could feel the thickening length of his member under the makeshift kilt he wore, and she rubbed herself against him, grinding her hips against his.

Nyxant's fingers curled against her scalp and he gasped at the sensation. He pulled her in tighter, his lips urgent against hers. He was like a drug, clouding her senses, sending her soaring and getting under her skin. If she let this get too far, she could become addicted to him.

She heard a rollicking *crack* coming from the water and wanted to ignore it, too caught up in Nyxant. But the thunder that followed made her step back. She looked out over the sea, expecting to see storm clouds billowing.

Instead she saw salvation. There was a small orbiter heading straight toward them.

Nyxant turned to take a look at where she stared. When he saw it, he cursed, the words untranslatable but the meaning clear. He jumped back and ran for his tent, grabbing his damp pants along the way.

Sarah stood frozen. She'd nearly resigned herself to being stuck on this planet. It was almost unbelievable that they had been found so quickly.

"Sarah, I—" Nyxant tried to tell her something, but the loud engines of the orbiter drowned him out.

In minutes, the orbiter had crossed the water to hover next to the escape vessel that had brought them to land. Judging by the sleek military design, this small ship wasn't a part of the Sky Chaser fleet. Had they prevailed on a local planet to lend aid?

The hatch came down and Sarah knew her questions would be answered eventually. She smiled over at Nyxant, but his face was grim.

Six of Nyxant's fellow warriors, Oscavians judging by their purple skin, marched out, guns at the ready. Two of the warriors pointed their weapons at her. On instinct, she raised her hands and froze.

What the hell? The words died in her throat before she could speak.

The head warrior ignored her and turned to Nyxant. They didn't point their guns at him.

"My lord, are you alright?" he asked.

His lord?

They might have been saved, but Sarah was more confused than ever.

7

SARAH HAD SEEN WORSE prison cells, but she'd never been a prisoner in one. Right now, she wasn't sure exactly what her status was. After the rescue, things had gone by in a blur.

Somehow, she'd ended up in a small but nicely appointed room. It had everything she could want: a bathroom with a small shower stall, a food processor that could whip up anything she could imagine, a small but sinfully soft bed, and a window that looked out into the inky blackness of space.

The only thing she was missing was a way out. After taking her time washing off the sand and accumulated dirt from Rex, she'd grabbed the first clothing she saw in the closet—another jumpsuit, this one blue—and tried placing her palm against the panel beside the door to open it up. A warning had flashed on the screen and the door had remained steadfastly shut. After trying a few more times, she'd given up.

And now she was stewing, trying to put the pieces together. They weren't on Sky Chaser 4. Obviously. This was a military grade vessel, at least from what she'd seen as she'd been walked to this room.

The men who'd rescued them had called Nyxant 'sire.' What *was* he? A prince? A king? A tyrant?

Right now he was gone, and she'd never realized that a person could burrow under her defenses so quickly that she'd miss him after only a few days together. At most they'd been separated for a few hours, but it felt like much longer. She was adrift, her anchor gone.

She need to pull herself together.

The view screen beside the food processor lit up, and a man she'd never seen before addressed her. Like Nyxant, his skin was that rich deep purple, but his hair hung in long dark braids past his shoulders and his eyes were twin pools of inky black, not the ice bright blue of her man.

"I do apologize for the inconvenience, Miss Gallagher," he said. If he knew her name, he must have spoken to Nyxant. At least she hoped that he had. He continued speaking before she could ask questions. "An escort will arrive shortly and everything shall be made clear." The man cut off the transmission, leaving her alone and even more confused.

A minute later, the door opened and a different man in black fatigues entered. "Follow me, please," he ordered, and stepped aside to let her pass through the door.

She walked out and asked, "Can you tell me where we're going?" But the soldier didn't answer.

In the hallway there were two more Oscavian warriors. The three soldiers led her down several seemingly identical gray hallways in silence. Sarah gave up on asking questions. After a few minutes, they arrived at a green door and the first warrior placed his palm on the sensor beside it. The door slid open and they directed her to walk in.

Nyxant stood looking out into space through a large window. His profile faced her, though he didn't turn to greet her when the door slid shut behind her. Any doubts about his nobility dissolved when she caught sight of him. He'd bathed and changed his clothing. But unlike her, he hadn't put on a simple jumpsuit.

He wore a long jacket that fell to mid-thigh, the fabric thick and beige, but with lavender designs carefully and subtly woven in. It was edged by a thin braid of gold thread as thick as her index finger. Below the jacket his breeches were tight, clinging to his muscular legs, and as he turned toward her, she caught a glimpse of a simple black shirt under the jacket. His hair had been pulled back and tied by another subtle gold braid.

If she'd seen him like this on the ship, she would have never assumed he was a warrior. She would have known him for a prince.

Sarah's mouth had to be hanging open from the look of Nyxant's satisfied smile. "Please, join me," he said.

She walked up to the window and stood beside him, almost reaching out for his hand. But the fine quality of his clothing and the implications of his rank, whatever it was, held her back. "So you're a..." she trailed off, unsure how to end her sentence.

He sighed and rattled off his titles like they were childhood embarrassments. "Lord of the

Fourth High Council, Brother to the crown prince, and son of Queen Nysaria." He stopped there and said, "There's more, but those are the important ones."

"Royalty?" He was the son of a queen and she was the daughter of no one. She knew nothing could last between them, but that was supposed to be because of distance, not because he might inherit a planet one day.

"I am sorry for the subterfuge," he said, truly sounding apologetic. "Planetside I could not..."

"Be sure I wasn't a really incompetent assassin?" The entire situation was absurd.

He laughed. "Perhaps not an assassin." He grew serious. "My head of security was overzealous in keeping you confined to your quarters."

The distance between them was too great. Sarah reached out and grabbed his hand. She needed to hold onto something right now. "What's going on?" she asked.

Nyxant looked at their entwined fingers and squeezed. "I did not think you'd be able to forgive me."

For the lie? She wanted to ask. Instead she said, "I'm working out the emotions." They were swirling around in her mind, keeping her off balance. "Right now I just want to understand."

He nodded and explained. "My people and I were on a diplomatic mission. In the course of our negotiations, things went wrong. Someone— my people are trying to figure out who— attempted to hijack the ship. They disabled *most* of the sirens above the Sky Chaser vessel."

"But not on my floor?" It would explain why no one else had ended up in that escape vessel.

"Our floor, *cavria*," he corrected. "There was a mistake in the bookings. My party meant to rent out the entire level. Due to a computer error, you were placed down the hall."

"So I'm just lucky?" She didn't know if she was being sarcastic.

Neither did Nyxant. "Would you call the last few days lucky?" he asked.

"I think I might." With Nyxant standing in front of her, it felt so true. She'd met the most amazing man she'd ever known. She'd kissed him on an abandoned beach a day after he'd saved her life. Lucky? She might have been blessed. The last few days were something that she would savor for the rest of her life.

Nyxant took a step closer and continued to

explain. "My warriors calculated where the ship landed and sent out the rescue vessel."

"And the negotiations?" she asked.

"Delayed for now." He smoothed her hair back behind her ear, and for a second, Sarah thought that he would kiss her. But he took a step back and said, "I have a proposition for you."

"Oh?" From his serious expression, she doubted he was about to make a wicked proposition. Though she wondered what she would say if he did.

"I have no wish to indenture you." He half-turned away from her and raised his hand up toward the window as if he were tracing the stars. "If you'd prefer, we will drop you off at the nearest travel hub with the resources to return home in the height of comfort."

That sounded tempting, but she wanted to know what else he was offering. "Or?" she asked.

Nyxant turned back toward her. Those blue eyes of his lit up with nascent hope. "We are negotiating with a human corporation about land rights. An Oscavian has joined their delegation to offer advice on protocol."

"And you want me to do the same for you?" She'd never considered being human a job qualification before, but right now, it might have just given her the opportunity of a lifetime.

He nodded. "Yes."

She wanted to grab it with both hands and jump headfirst at the chance to take this job. But if she was being completely honest with herself, it wasn't really what she wanted from him. It took courage to find the will to say it, but she'd faced down a monster in the jungle. She could say what she was beginning to feel. "That wasn't the kind of proposition I was hoping for," she confessed.

His pupils expanded, the darkness blotting out the blue as he sucked in a breath. "Did you want something more like this?" The distance between them dissolved and suddenly he was flush against her, chest to chest, his arms wrapped around her tightly. His head dipped down and he captured her lips, tasting her, conquering her, claiming her. Sarah opened up to him, heated by his taste.

All too quickly he pulled back, leaving Sarah's heart pounding and her blood singing. "Oh. Wow," was all she could say.

"You are a remarkable woman, Sarah Gallagher." His mouth hugged the syllables of her name, caressing her with his special pronunciation. "And I do not want you far from my side."

She didn't know what it meant. She was a human and he was Oscavian. She was a commoner and he was a prince. In any sane world, there were uncrossable galaxies between them. But right now, she was in his arms with the imprint of his lips still hot against her own.

She'd left the sane world behind the minute she'd been ejected from Sky Chaser 4.

If she stepped back now, she'd regret it forever. So she smiled up at him, heart swelling, and said, "I've always wanted to see the universe."

Drakarn Mates

A HARSH DESERT PLANET. Stranded humans. Draconic aliens. A match made in… well, somewhere.

Claimed by the Drakarn Warrior Lord
Echoes of Fire
Scorched by Fate
Fated to the Drakarn Commander
Chained to the Champion
Beast of Ash and Blood

Dragon Brides

Dragon Princes. Fierce Women. Love.
Fated mates, fierce women, and dragon princes
are ready to find their mates.
Also available in audio!

Crux

Ranger

Saber

Cipher

Storm

Drake

Asher

Knox

Flint

Pine

Guarded by the Shifter

Werewolf. Bodyguard. Mate.
The origins of these shifters are shrouded in
mystery, but they're determined to protect their
mates from any harm that comes their way.
Also available in audio!

Hunting Season
On the Prowl
Stalking Magic
Hungry for the Wolf
Wolf Cursed (novella)
Wolf's Temptation

———

Stealing the Alpha

The thief takes what she wants, but the alpha keeps what's his...
Join shifter thief Mel as she clashes with lion alpha Luke in an explosive trilogy of two opposites who can't keep away from one another.
Also available in audio!
The Alpha Heist
Entangled with the Thief
In the Alpha's Bed

———

Alien Mates: Planet Exile

Guerran is no place for pretty human women. But these alien heroes will protect their mates!
Also available in audio!

Exile's Hunter
Exile's Adored

———

Zulir Warrior Mates

Kidnapped humans. Alien Warriors. Electric wings.
The Zulir Warrior Mates series brings you human heroines and heroes abducted from Earth who find love – and wings! – with the alien warriors who rescue them.
Also available in audio!

Synnr's Saint
Synnr's Hope
Synnr's Spark
Synnr's Kiss
Synnr's Ride

Mated to the Alien

Fated Mate Alien Romance
Detyens are doomed to die young if they don't find their fated mates.
Follow along as these mated pairs fight off aliens, corrupt dictators, prejudiced humans, pirates, and more! The books can be read or listened to in any order, though some characters show up in multiple stories.
Select books available in audio.
Pick a book and jump into the action today!

Ruwen

Tyral

Stoan

Cyborg

Krayter

Kayleb

Shayn

Braxtyn

Doryan

Dekon

Detyen Warriors

Detya was destroyed a hundred years ago. These doomed warriors are out to find justice... and their mates.

The Detyen Warriors series brings you kick butt heroines, alpha alien heroes, fated mates, and relationships strong enough to span the galaxy!

The entire series is also available in audio!

Soulless

Ruthless

Heartless

Faultless

Endless

Detyen Warrior Outcasts

Fated Mate Alien Romance

These doomed warriors were abandoned by their people and live on the edge. Their mates hold the key to their salvation.

Pick a book and jump into the action today!

Also available in audio!

Dangerous Bond

Intrepid Bond
Wayward Bond

Alien Holiday Romance

Christmas… in space????
These alien holiday romances look beyond Earth's
winter holidays and ring in the season across the
galaxy!
Select titles available in audio.
Snowed in with the Alien Beast
The Alien's Winter Gift
The Alien Reindeer's Wild Ride
Trapped with her Alien Mate

Alien Outlaws

**Outlaws, schemes, and love… it's all there
in the Alien Outlaws series…**
Andie Munster is sick of life on Ixilta, the planet
she got dumped on after being abducted from
Earth six years ago. And when the mysterious and

dangerous Xandr shows up looking for a way off the planet, she's half-prisoner, half-co-conspirator in a wild rush to escape.

Also available in audio!

Rogue Alien's Escape

Rogue Alien's Woman

Rogue Alien's Secret

Rogue Alien's Legacy

———

Find more by Kate Rudolph at www.katerudolph.net

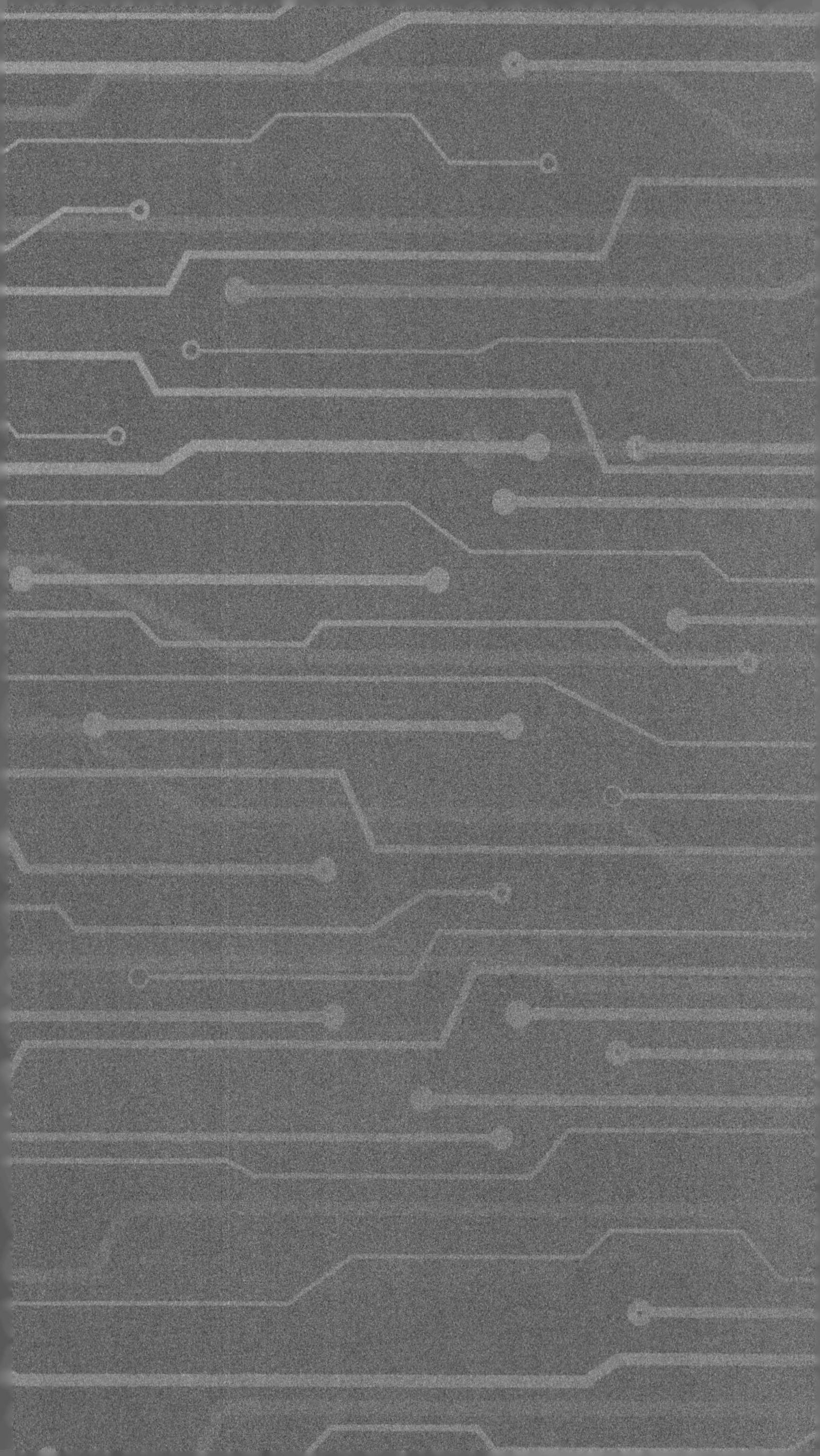

ABOUT KATE RUDOLPH

KATE RUDOLPH IS a paranormal and sci-fi romance writer who lives in Indiana. She loves writing about kick butt heroines and the steamy heroes who love them. She's been devouring romance novels since she was too young to be reading them and had to hide her books so no one would take them away. She couldn't imagine a better job in this world than writing romances and sharing them with her fellow readers.

If you enjoyed this story, please consider leaving a review.

ARE YOU A STARR HUNTRESS?

DO you love to read sci fi romance about strong, independent women and the sexy alien males who love them?

Starr Huntress is a coalition of the brightest Starrs in romance banding together to explore uncharted territories.

If you like your men horny- maybe literally- and you're equal opportunity skin color- because who doesn't love a guy with blue or green skin?- then join us as we dive into swashbuckling space adventure, timeless romance, and lush alien landscapes.

www.ingramcontent.com/pod-product-compliance
Lightning Source LLC
Chambersburg PA
CBHW061250140726
47998CB00006B/2183